The
Cowboy
Kid

by A.H. Benjamin and
Garyfallia Leftheri

W
FRANKLIN WATTS
LONDON • SYDNEY

First published in 2015 by
Franklin Watts
338 Euston Road
London
NW1 3BH

Franklin Watts Australia
Level 17/207 Kent Street
Sydney
NSW 2000

FSC
www.fsc.org
MIX
Paper from
responsible sources
FSC® C104740

Text © A.H. Benjamin 2015
Illustration © Garyfallia Leftheri 2015

The rights of A.H. Benjamin to be identified as the
author and Garyfallia Leftheri as the illustrator of this Work
have been asserted in accordance with the Copyright, Designs
andPatents Act, 1988.

A CIP catalogue record for this book is available
from the British Library.

ISBN 978 1 4451 3946 3 (hbk)
ISBN 978 1 4451 3949 4 (pbk)
ISBN 978 1 4451 3948 7 (library ebook)
ISBN 978 1 4451 3947 0 (ebook)

Series Editor: Jackie Hamley
Series Advisor: Catherine Glavina
Series Designer: Peter Scoulding

Printed in China

Franklin Watts is a divison of
Hachette Children's Books,
an Hachette UK company.
www.hachette.co.uk

Max wanted to be
a cowboy.

He got a lasso and started to practise.

He swung the lasso
over his head and …

Oops! He caught himself.

"You'll get better," smiled Mum.

Max aimed at the gatepost and …

9

Oops! He caught the cat.

"Bad luck," said Dad.

Max aimed at a
flower pot and ...

Oops! He caught his uncle.

"Keep practising, Max!"
his uncle said.

Max decided to help his
sister catch her puppy
and …

Oops! He caught his sister.
"Max, no!" panted his sister.

"Will I ever be a cowboy?"
thought Max, sadly.

One day, Max went to a
country show with Dad.
He took his lasso
with him.

Suddenly, a big bull came charging towards them.

The gate to his field had been left wide open.

Max aimed his lasso at
the bull and …

Oops! He caught the gate. Max pulled hard and the gate closed just in time.

27

"Well done!" cried Dad.

"Three cheers for the Cowboy Kid" shouted everyone.

Puzzle 1

Put these pictures in the correct order.
Now tell the story in your own words.
Can you think of a different ending?

Puzzle 2

excited   dismayed
thrilled

annoyed   jolly
cross

Choose the words which best describe Max and which best describe his sister in the pictures. Can you think of any more?

Answers

Puzzle 1

The correct order is:

1e, 2c, 3a, 4f, 5b, 6d

Puzzle 2

Max   The correct words are excited, thrilled.
The incorrect word is dismayed.

Sister   The correct words are angry, cross.
The incorrect word is jolly.

Look out for more stories: